TESSA KRAILLING

The Oakhollow Mystery

Illustrated by
Amanda Wood

OXFORD
UNIVERSITY PRESS

OXFORD
UNIVERSITY PRESS

Great Clarendon Street, Oxford OX2 6DP

Oxford University Press is a department of the University of Oxford.
It furthers the University's objective of excellence in research, scholarship,
and education by publishing worldwide in

Oxford New York
Athens Auckland Bangkok Bogotá Buenos Aires Calcutta
Cape Town Chennai Dar es Salaam Delhi Florence Hong Kong Istanbul
Karachi Kuala Lumpur Madrid Melbourne Mexico City Mumbai
Nairobi Paris São Paulo Shanghai Singapore Taipei Tokyo Toronto Warsaw

and associated companies in Berlin Ibadan

Oxford is a trade mark of Oxford University Press
in the UK and in certain other countries

First published 2001

British Library Cataloguing in Publication Data
Data available

ISBN 0 19 917425 3

Printed in Hong Kong

Available in packs

Year 3 / Primary 4 Pack of Six (one of each book) ISBN 0 19 917427 X
Year 3 / Primary 4 Class Pack (six of each book) ISBN 0 19 917428 8

For Megan Chastney,
with love

Contents

FRAGILE

1

Moving Day

Megan woke up with the feeling that Something Scary was about to happen. For a moment she couldn't remember what it was. Then she saw the suitcases packed with her clothes, the boxes filled with books and her collection of china ornaments.

Oh, now she remembered!

This was her last day in her old

home. Never again would she wake up in this cosy room with its primrose-coloured walls. Never again would she lie in bed listening to the sound of boats chugging up and down the busy river. Never again would she…

"Meg?" Her younger brother Davy stuck his head round the door. "You're still in bed! Have you forgotten we're moving house today?"

She groaned. "No, I haven't forgotten."

"Hurry up, then." He disappeared.

Megan slid down beneath the quilt. She wished she could stay in bed for ever. She felt safe in this friendly little flat where she had lived all her life. She didn't want to move to a strange house on the other side of town.

A house called Oakhollow...

"Wake up, Lazybones!" Mum came into the room. "Dad and Davy are already having breakfast."

Megan slid even further beneath the quilt. "Mum, do we have to?"

"Do we have to what?"

"Move to Oakhollow." Even the name scared her a little, although she didn't know why. "I like this flat. Why can't we stay where we are?"

"Oh, Megan!" Mum pulled back the curtains, letting in the sunlight. "We'll have so much more space in the new house. And a garden! You know how much your father has

longed to have a garden."

"Yes, but... but it won't be home, will it?" She found it hard to put her feelings into words. "This is our home. It'll seem strange living somewhere else."

"At first, perhaps. But you'll soon get used to it." Mum sat down on the edge of the bed. "Things can't stay the same for ever, you know. This flat is far too small for us now, especially with a new baby on the way. It's time to move on."

Megan had forgotten about the baby. That would be another big change in their lives, but a nice one this time. And of course it would be far better for the baby to play outside in the garden, breathing in lots of fresh air.

"Try to think of it as an adventure." Mum jumped to her feet. "Now, if you don't hurry up the removal men will take the bed with you still in it."

Left alone, Megan took one last look out of her bedroom window. From their third-floor flat she could see right across the rooftops to the docks. She loved to watch the cranes loading and unloading the huge container ships, the ferries and big luxury liners leaving for ports all over the world. She even loved the damp, oily, spicy smell of the river that came wafting through the open window.

Oh, how she would miss her old home!

Next morning she awoke with the feeling that Something Scary had happened. For a moment she couldn't remember what it was. Then she opened her eyes and saw that everything looked different. The room was bigger, the window had moved, the door was on the wrong side of the room. Where was she?

Oakhollow!

She sat up with a start. Yesterday had been chaotic – Mum and Dad rushing about, their furniture being put in the wrong rooms, everyone getting crosser and crosser. By the evening they were so tired they had fallen into bed and gone straight to sleep.

But today was a new day. For the first time she began to feel excited.

Mum was right, moving house was an adventure.

She jumped out of bed and went over to the window. What a difference! No river, no docks, just a long, narrow back garden with a

high hedge. And it was so quiet. All she could hear was the faint hum of traffic along the distant main road.

"You awake, Meg?" Davy's head appeared round the door. "I've got something to show you." He came into the room, clutching a piece of paper.

"What is it?"

"A note. I found it stuck inside the cupboard door in my room." He held it out to her. "Go on, read it."

She stared down at the bold black writing. In capital letters it said:

THIS HOUSE IS DANGEROUS. GO AWAY.

2

Something Spooky

"What do you think it means?" Davy asked.

Megan read the note again, trying to make sense of it. How could this house possibly be dangerous? And why was someone telling them to go away when they'd only just arrived?

Davy went on, "Last night I was

too tired to put things away, but this morning I opened the cupboard door and there it was. Who do you think wrote it?" He looked suddenly fearful. "Maybe there's a ghost?"

"Don't be daft. Ghosts don't write letters, they just clank their chains and make moaning noises." Megan handed the note back to Davy. "Let's get dressed and go downstairs."

"OK, beat you to the bathroom."

As soon as he had gone, Megan opened the cupboard. To her relief there was nothing stuck on the inside of the door. No warning note, no message telling her to go away. She decided to put the whole thing out of her head. No point in letting it spoil their first day in the new house.

At breakfast Davy showed the note first to Mum and then to Dad.

Mum read it and laughed. “Of course this house isn’t dangerous! We wouldn’t have come to live here if it was.”

Dad said, "I expect it was left by the family who've just moved out. One of the kids, most likely." He turned to Mum. "Did Mrs Barker have any children?"

"One, I think," said Mum. "A boy."

"There you are, then." Dad tossed the note back to Davy. "I expect he used to sleep in your room and left it behind as a joke."

"Not a very friendly sort of joke," said Megan.

"No, it wasn't," Mum agreed. "Never mind, the Barkers don't live here any more. We do. Now, if you've finished breakfast why don't you two go outside and explore?"

Megan grinned. "What you really mean is you don't want us under your feet."

"Right first time!" said Mum.

It felt strange to step straight out into a garden instead of walking down flights of stairs. Megan stood still, gazing at the square green lawn surrounded by flower beds. Beyond that, half-hidden behind some rose bushes, was a vegetable plot and a wooden shed. And right at the far end of the garden stood the ancient hollow oak tree that gave the house its name.

"I'm going to look inside the shed." Davy sped off.

Megan followed more slowly, stopping to sniff the roses on the way. Some of them had a gorgeous scent while others hardly smelled at all.

"It's locked," said Davy when she reached the shed. "And there's a note pinned to the door. It says: DANGER. KEEP OUT."

"That's silly," said Megan. "How can it be dangerous? It's only an ordinary old wooden shed."

"Maybe there's a wild animal inside." Davy peered through the window. "No, just a lot of forks and spades and stuff."

"I expect Dad asked Mrs Barker to leave them behind," said Megan. "He hasn't got any tools of his own. This is the first time he's ever had a garden."

She wandered over to the oak tree. It must be very, very old. And how did it come to be hollow? Perhaps it had been struck by lightning. Fascinated, she peered into the hole.

Her eye was caught by something white. She reached inside and pulled out a piece of paper. It said:

THIS TREE IS HAUNTED.
KEEP AWAY.

"What is it?" asked Davy, coming up behind her.

"Only another of those stupid notes." Hastily, she crumpled it up.

"But what does it say?"

"Nothing important." She stuffed it into her jeans pocket. "Let's go and ask Dad if we can have the key to the shed."

"OK." He sped back up the garden.

Megan touched the crumpled

note in her pocket. Just another joke – or a serious warning that there was something spooky about Oakhollow? Perhaps Davy had been right about the ghost after all?

3

A Ghost in the Garden?

Dad searched through the keys he had been given by the estate agent. "Nothing here that looks as if it might fit the shed," he said. "Did you say it's full of garden tools?"

Megan nodded. "We thought you must have asked Mrs Barker to leave them behind."

"No, it never occurred to me," said Dad. "But if she doesn't want them back we can certainly make good use of them. Show me."

They made their way back down the garden.

As they passed the vegetable plot Dad said, "Look at those runner beans! I bet they taste better than the ones we get from the supermarket. We'll pick some later and have them for supper."

Megan glanced at the long green pods hanging from a framework of bamboo canes. She had never seen runner beans actually growing before. Would they really taste different?

Dad peered through the shed window. "Hey, you're right! There's even a lawnmower. Are you sure the door's locked?"

"Yes, and there's a note saying keep out," said Davy.

Dad tried the handle, but the door stayed shut. Frowning, he read the note.

"Looks like the work of our phantom note-writer again." He unpinned it and screwed it up. "Luckily, Mrs Barker left us her new address and telephone number. I'll ask her to let me have the key as soon as possible."

Megan wished he hadn't mentioned phantoms. A phantom was a ghost, and she was trying hard not to think about ghosts. It was bad enough living in a house that might be haunted. But a ghost in the garden? She shuddered. Now that was really spooky!

They spent the rest of the day indoors, unpacking and sorting out their belongings. By the evening they felt tired and very, very hungry.

"Let's stop," said Mum. "I'll get us something to eat."

"Good idea," said Dad. He handed Megan a plastic bag. "Why don't you go and pick those beans? I just fancy some with my supper."

Davy jumped up. "I'll help you, Meggie."

But when they arrived at the vegetable plot they had a shock.

No beans!

"Where've they gone?" asked Megan. "There were lots here this morning, I saw them."

"Perhaps they fell off." Davy searched the ground. "No, there's nothing here."

"Somebody must have picked them." A shiver ran down Megan's spine. Did ghosts eat runner beans?

"Hey, look at this!" Davy pointed to a freshly dug patch of earth behind the beanpoles. "I'm sure that wasn't there this morning."

Megan stared at it. "But – but nobody can get into the garden without walking through the house. We'd have seen them."

"Well, somebody's been here. I wonder if they left any footprints." He started searching the path leading to the shed.

Megan looked uneasily round the garden. This was getting spookier and spookier!

"Meg, come and look," called Davy. He pointed to the shed door. "There's a key in the lock."

She stared at it in amazement. Where had it come from? It certainly hadn't been there earlier in the day.

She tried the handle. The door opened easily.

They stepped inside. The shed was amazingly tidy with forks, spades, rakes, hoes all neatly stored

on hooks. Pinned next to them was a note:

TOUCH THESE TOOLS AND YOU'RE DEAD!

Davy said, "That wasn't there before either. I'd have seen it when I looked through the window." He looked scared. "Meg, are you sure ghosts can't write letters?"

Megan shook her head. After all, if the messages had been left by the boy who used to live here they should have stopped. The Barkers must be miles away by now. But whoever – or whatever – had written those messages and unlocked the shed door was still here!

4

The Phantom Gardener

They burst into the kitchen.

"Dad! Mum!" called Megan. "The key to the shed's come back!"

Dad looked puzzled. "But I haven't had time to telephone Mrs Barker yet."

"And someone's nicked all our runner beans," panted Davy.

Mum handed Dad the telephone. "Call Mrs Barker now," she said. "I think we need to know what's going on."

He dialled the number and waited.

"No reply," he said at last. "She must be out. I'll try again later."

"Meantime you kids had better go and clean yourselves up," said Mum. "Supper will be ready in half an hour – with or without runner beans."

Megan went upstairs slowly, still thinking about the ghost. As she stood in front of the mirror, brushing her hair, she glanced out of the window. Was it her imagination or could she see something moving around at the bottom of the garden?

Something white…

Her heart thumping, she went closer to the window and peered out. Yes, there was definitely something down by the vegetable plot. But it wasn't a ghost.

It was a boy in a white T-shirt!

Without stopping to think, she raced downstairs and into the garden. "Hey, you!" she called. "Who are you?"

The boy swung round. "I'm Alex Barker. Who are you?"

"My name's Megan." She stopped to catch her breath. "But you don't live here any more. So what are you doing in our garden?"

He shrugged. "I only wanted to make sure nobody's been messing up my vegetables."

"*Your* vegetables?" She stared at him. "Was it you that picked our runner beans?"

"*My* runner beans." He stuck out his chin. "I grew them."

"And was it you that left all those messages?" she asked.

He glowered at her. "What if I did?"

Megan giggled. "We thought it was a ghost. Oh, at first we wondered if it might be you, but when the messages kept on coming we couldn't understand it. We thought you'd be miles away by now."

"Hardly miles," he said scornfully. "We've only moved to the other side of town, down by the docks."

"The docks?" She was amazed. "But that's where we came from! We used to live in a flat near the river."

He groaned. "I hate it there. It's boring."

"No, it isn't. It's the most exciting place in the world. I didn't want to move away but we've got a new baby coming so we needed more room." She asked curiously, "Didn't you want to move either?"

He shook his head. "I've lived at Oakhollow all my life. But when our dad left us, Mum said we couldn't afford to stay here any more. So now we're living in a small house with no garden, just a backyard." He pulled a disgusted face. "You can't grow proper vegetables in a backyard!"

Megan was beginning to understand. "So that's why you left your tools behind. And all those notes telling us to go away. You wanted to scare us off so that you could carry on working in your garden."

Alex looked a little ashamed. "Yeah, well . . . I'm sorry about the notes. I guess I got a bit carried away."

"But how did you get in?" she asked.

"I squeezed through the hedge," he said. "My mum's next door, collecting some stuff she left with our old neighbour. They're good friends, so I reckoned I could come and do some gardening whenever we visited."

At that moment Mum, Dad and Davy came racing towards them. "What's going on? Who's this? Megan, are you all right?"

"I'm fine." She explained quickly who Alex was and what he was doing in their garden. "His mum's visiting next door. That's why you couldn't get her on the phone, Dad."

"Well, at least we've solved the mystery of our phantom gardener!" He looked hard at Alex. "Tell me, young man, is it just the vegetable plot you're interested in – or the whole garden?"

Alex went red. "Just the vegetable plot."

"In that case," said Dad, "I suggest we come to an agreement. If you let me borrow your gardening tools, I'll let you come and work on your vegetable plot whenever you like."

Alex stared at him. "Do you mean it?"

"Of course I mean it." Dad held out his hand. "Bargain?"

"Bargain!" Grinning, Alex shook his hand. "And we can share the vegetables. I always grow too many anyway."

"Actually," said Mum, "we were hoping to have some runner beans for our supper."

"Wait here." Alex disappeared through the hedge.

Dad winked at the others. "I suggest we go and start boiling the water to cook our beans."

"I'll stay and collect them," said Megan.

Mum, Dad and Davy went back to the house, leaving Megan alone by the vegetable plot. It was odd how things had worked out, she thought, the Barkers going to live on the other side of town, while they had come to Oakhollow. All they had really done was change places.

Alex burst through the hedge, holding a plastic bag full of beans. “Will this be enough?” he asked.

"Plenty, thanks," said Megan. "Alex, I've been thinking. You say you didn't want to leave this house. Well, I didn't want to leave the river. So could I come and visit you sometimes?"

Alex looked first surprised, then pleased. "Yeah, OK."

"Alex?" called a voice from the other side of the hedge. "Where are you? It's time we went home."

"Coming," he called back. He pulled a face at Megan. "Home!"

She pulled a face back in sympathy. "I expect it'll take us both a while to get used to living somewhere different. Bye, Alex. See you soon."

"Bye, Megan." He disappeared through the hedge.

Slowly, she carried the beans back to the house. What was it Mum had said yesterday morning, before they left their old flat? Something about things not staying the same for ever...

Maybe she was right. After all, once their new baby arrived everything would be different!

About the author

I wrote my first story at the age of four. I always knew I wanted to be a writer, but it was many years before my first book was published. Since then I have written over thirty books for children of all ages. Best of all, I like writing mystery stories.

I usually start by asking myself the question, "What if...?" For example, what if you moved into a new house and found a message that said "This house is dangerous. Go away."? Could the house be haunted? What a mystery!